THE STEWARDESS'S DIARY - PART ONE

CANADA

S.M. PRATT

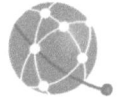

The Stewardess's Diary - Part One: Canada
Copyright © 2015 by S.M. Pratt

Last updated January 25th, 2020
Editing by Samantha Marie

ISBN: 978-0-9940630-4-5 (e-book)

ISBN: 978-1-988639-20-8 (paperback)

I'M CHARLIE, a veteran pilot for a major international airline that shall remain nameless for reasons you'll soon come to understand.

A year ago, while waiting for my flight to London in the airline's lounge at one of America's largest hubs, I discovered a special and highly personal journal among my belongings. How it happened, I'll never know, but the beautiful brown leather notebook nonetheless appeared in my briefcase at some point between the time I left my New York penthouse apartment and arrived at the airport lounge.

Perhaps it was a mix-up at security, or some devious stewardess with sly hand skills, but I've since become obsessed with the person who wrote that diary, her stories, and—to be blunt—her unconventional sex life.

My best friend—let's call him Bob—is one of my regular co-pilots. Bob advised me to forget about the journal and ignore my hunch to track down its rightful owner. After my initial reading of her hand-written accounts, the part of me who's loyal to the airline and wants the best for our passengers certainly needed to find that stewardess and expel her from our company—or whatever airline she's with. This woman is surely a threat to any crew with her irreverent disregard for our uniforms, her sexual behavior with passengers and airline employees, and the way she ignores regulations. She should clearly be punished for her conduct...

But after reading and re-reading each one of her journal entries, another, more animal part of me has grown fond of her complete lack of boundaries, her willingness to experiment, and her ravenous sexual appetite.

I've had my fair share of illicit affairs with female flight attendants and co-pilots, but none of them were interesting enough to be granted a second fuck by yours truly, let alone be courted or considered for a long-term relationship. But the woman who's filled so many pages with delicate calligraphy and salacious words deserves my full attention. She's certainly maintained it well past the time I closed the cover of her journal—again and again.

Imagining how her naiveté was gradually—and most willingly—robbed from her was simply... enthralling. She's been haunting my wet dreams.

Now, every time I see an unknown stewardess, I wonder if *she's* the one.

After many conversations with Bob over the past months during our overseas flights, I've come to share some of her journal entries with him. He agrees that I need to locate her. If not for the airline's sake or to satisfy my personal curiosity, then for the mere reason that I could stop obsessing about her and resume paying attention to my actual job: piloting giant aircrafts and safely getting passengers from point A to point B.

The following short stories record my obsession toward her. There are ten in total. Each installment contains my mystery stewardess's original journal entries for a specific location, followed by my own experiences in trying to track her down. You'll discover what (and whom) I did in an effort to identify and locate my stewardess based on the clues she's left in her diary. You can read the episodes in any order, but they'll probably make more sense if you start from the beginning and follow along as I attempt to find her.

And, just to be clear, these stories should *not* land in the hands of any prude or underage person. Some are just romantic, sensual, or highly erotic, while others are immoral, perverse, and possibly even illegal in some parts of the world.

Ah, the things I'll do to this mystery stewardess when I finally encounter her in the flesh!

I'm hard just thinking about it...

Yours truly,

Capt. Charlie
Undisclosed Airline

PART ONE

THE STEWARDESS'S ENTRIES

2:29 A.M.

AT LAST, I got to take a break from walking up and down the aisle. Most of the passengers in economy class were asleep and giving their service button a break. Most except for a workaholic in 8A and a musty-mustached man in 14D who kept winking at me.

How stupid was I to wear brand new heels on a red-eye flight? My feet and legs are killing me! If I don't have blisters yet, they're coming. That's for sure.

But these black babies look fantastic and I enjoy being a little taller.

Maybe I shouldn't have bought into the marketing hype, but high heels did make me feel sexier... and happier. And after my disastrous weekend getaway with Stupid-Self-Centered-Sam, I needed to take any emotional, mental, or shoe-related compensation I could get.

My sense of self-worth had to rise from this muddy bottom, and it had recently gone up by exactly three inches.

ARGH!

Musty-Mustached-Man-in-14D suggested (for the second time) that his ticket included entry to the mile-high club.

It was the only part of the job I didn't like.

Having a hottie flirt with me was always enjoyable, of course. But being hit on by a man who physically grossed me out and made me want to Febreze the heck out of the entire plane... Forcing myself to be polite and smile at him was just...

But thankfully, Alex, a tall red-headed stewardess I'd flown with before, graciously took him off my hands a minute ago.

I stayed within earshot while she chit-chatted with him.

Her exact words were impossible to recall, but she was nice and thoughtful. She certainly knew how to serve shit on a tray with a smile. She even got thanked for it.

Incredible.

I headed toward the back of the plane, a large smile on my face, shaking my head.

"Alex, I owe you one," I told her when she joined me back in the galley.

"No worries. I know how to handle those guys," she said. Alex lifted her eyebrows before continuing. "Not to toot my own horn, but I know how to manipulate most men to get what I want."

3:05 A.M.

I BUSIED myself seeing if there was trash or empty water bottles to get rid of, but my thoughts kept spinning back to Self-Centered-Sam.

"If only I had your ways with men," I told Alex. "Maybe I wouldn't be stuck spending my next over-nighter alone in a hotel room."

"Stop whining and move on with your life," she said, pouring herself a cup of coffee.

"But I thought he was the right guy for me. I liked him. I actually thought we were going somewhere, you know?"

Her big green eyes wide open, Alex stayed motionless for a second before shaking her head. She sipped more of her coffee, staring down the aisle, then at me. She sighed, shook her head again, then finally spoke. "What the heck happened? You might as well get it off your chest."

"I don't know," I said, mentally debating whether talking about it would help or make things worse.

"Come on," she persisted in-between sips. "Might as well pour your little heart out because I'll never ask about your love life again. You know me." Alex paused, raised her palm as if to stop the words she'd just let out, and then continued. "I'll never ask about your romantic life, but I reserve the right to ask about your sexual adventures."

I could feel my cheeks flush.

Talk about my sex life with her?

Then again, I needed to vent. Plus, we had a few hours to kill before landing.

She nudged me, her eyebrows raised, then walked away for a second to get rid of her empty coffee cup.

My inner debate continued, with logic taking the upper hand over my shyness and need for privacy.

Alex has politely offered her kind ear. It's now or never. Who knows? Maybe she can help me understand where I went wrong?

She came back and leaned against the bulkhead, her eyes locked on me.

"I don't even know where to begin..." I started, then let out a long breath. *How can I summarize it all?* "To make a long story short—"

She flicked her fingers against my shoulder. "No way. I want all the details. Especially the juicy bits."

"Not sure about that. We'll see. It all started when we arrived at the campground near Banff."

"Which one?" she asked.

"You've probably never heard of it. It's not even posted on any of the maps I've seen."

She tilted her head. "Try me."

"Slanted Pine Roads, I think."

Alex twisted her face for a second.

Is she trying to pinpoint that campsite on the map of her mental atlas?

"You're right: no idea. Never heard of that one. Continue."

"Doesn't matter anyway. Sam knew where it was, so he headed directly to the little building at the entrance so he could check in and pay for one of the sites where his pickup truck would fit."

"You guys weren't camping in an RV?"

"No, just the back of his truck. Believe me, I'd have preferred a tent. At least the ground wouldn't have been so hard. Anyway, he stayed in there for a few minutes. I remained outside and hung around the truck, trying to get cellphone reception—which was impossible. He finally walked out of the building and returned to our vehicle, then we drove and parked at one of the campsites. There weren't many. Maybe twenty-five or so—"

"But please tell me there were showers, right? Regular toilets and showers with running water?"

"Of course. He knew better than to take me camping without the basic necessities. He was an ass in many ways, but he was still a gentleman... Well, at that point he hadn't proven otherwise yet."

"So, what happened?"

I stopped as I noticed a tired-looking passenger walking toward us. *Probably wants to use the bathroom at the back of the plane.*

Alex frowned, her palms flipped upward in a silent WTF. I pointed my chin at the man.

She turned around. "Ah," she said.

We stayed quiet for a couple of minutes. Out of boredom, I yet again tidied up the food preparation area.

A loud flushing sound echoed from the nearby toilet, and I waited for the passenger to exit and return to his seat, out of earshot, before finally continuing. "So, it was all fine and good. We went for a walk around the site. It was nice. The smell of the forest, the quietness of it all, the chirping sounds and everything... We hiked up some random path. Must have been on it for about an hour before we reached a small river. Beautiful, but holy cow was the water cold!"

"You swam in it?"

"Hell no! But Sam did. I don't know why. Anyway, after he came out, he was freezing. Obviously. So I... warmed him up again," I said, tilting my head to the side.

"I said I wanted to hear all the juicy bits," she whispered, although her expression was silently yelling at me, ordering me to divulge everything.

I popped my eyes at her. "I promise to give you some, the important ones, but let's just say that we had a... quickie by the river and some body heat got transferred where it mattered."

"Seriously, you've got to work on that. If that's as exciting as your story gets, I don't want to hear any more."

"Alex, just be patient!" I exclaimed in a hushed tone. "So, about an hour and a half later, we were back in the truck. It was already getting pretty cool by then. He told me he was going to start a fire, so I got changed into my jeans and sweater. He said he was heading out to buy a pack of logs. That was all fine and good. The chilly mountain air was getting to me, so after waiting for him for what felt like an eternity—or at least thirty minutes—I made my way to the reception building to see what was taking him so long. I walked in on him flirting with a cute twenty-something girl wearing a large sweater and possibly shorts, although I couldn't tell. Long legs, wool socks, and hiking boots were all I could see. I guess she was the campsite employee."

"Ooh la la!" Alex said.

"Yes. I think that's when our romantic getaway took a left turn. I greeted them both. He picked up the stack of fire wood and said he'd be right out, but I saw him lean toward her and whisper something in her ear. I should have known something was up, but I didn't want to see it. Anyway, we headed back to our campsite together. He then carried on explaining himself. Telling me some bullshit about how they grew up in the same town."

"What? In Canada?"

"Yeah! I thought he was American. Tells you how much I knew about him. Not that his nationality mattered, but I simply didn't know anything about this guy. So we started drinking beer (he had brought a cooler full). He got busy cooking potatoes and steaks on the fire. That girl from the registration building kept patrolling around the path that connected all campsites. Every time she drove by in her pickup truck, she'd smile and wave at us, although I suspected she mostly waved at him."

"So... Are you telling me that smiles and hand gestures were the only things that happened? That's lame."

"No, no! Patience, Alex. Don't get your panties in a big wet knot! So, we were cuddling by the fire, trying to stay warm, but I was exhausted and wanted to go to bed. We moved to the back of his truck, made love, then I fell asleep."

"Why am I listening to you? You don't stand a chance in Top-Sexy-Weekend contenders. You must be boring as hell in the sack."

Who is she to insinuate what I'm like in bed?

I did my best to ignore her insult and continued with my story. "That night was pretty dull. Had to stick to missionary position so the truck wouldn't rock too much and bother nearby campers. I woke up a little later and realized he wasn't in his sleeping bag. So, since I had to pee anyway—those nights are damn cool in the mountains—I put on a sweater and jeans and headed out of the truck. My eyes took a second to acclimate to the dark night sky, but then a cloud moved out of the way and the full moon lit my path. I was heading toward the bathroom when I noticed the campground vehicle a few feet from our site, on the main path. I wouldn't have thought anything of it, except that it was moving... to a certain cadence, if you catch my drift."

"Someone was fucking the campsite employee in there?" Alex asked, looking like saliva was about to come out of her mouth.

"Yeah. So, putting two and two together, Sam not being asleep next to me and the rocking motion of the pickup truck... I felt an urge to go and see. The windows were fogged up and a woman's moans were becoming less and less discreet. Then a hand reached toward the window and landed flat on it before slowly dropping down, clearing enough of the condensation and letting enough moonlight in for me to see inside."

Alex's green eyes were glued on me. "And?" she asked.

"It was the campsite employee alright, and I would have recognized that tight ass and left-slanted cock in any line-up. It was *my* Sam, going at her, just a few feet from where he'd left me to sleep after making love to me."

"Oh no! What did you do?"

"What do you think I did?"

"Oooh!" A large grin appeared on Alex's face. Her eyes had never been rounder. "You slammed a baseball bat on the windshield? Smashed the head lights? Did you call her supervisor? Oh, I know! You did something much, much better..." She paused and grabbed me by the arm before whispering her last guess in my ear. "Did you join them?"

I pulled away from her and shook my head. "What's wrong with you?"

A throat-clearing sound made me turn around. A teenage kid was standing there, wanting some water. Based on his glazed-over eyes, he hadn't heard a word of what I'd been saying. *Good.*

I grabbed a plastic glass and filled it with water, then handed it to him. "Here you go, dear," I said, and then waited until he was seated again to turn and look at Alex once more.

"No. None of that," I answered. "I went back to the truck and pretended to be sleeping when he snuck back in."

She flipped her hands up. "Seriously. What the fuck is wrong with you?"

"Nothing. I was upset. I was really upset—and I still am to be honest—but I needed to first process the information in my head before confronting him. I don't believe we need to dramatize everything."

"Well, your life would be a lot more interesting, at least sexually speaking, if you were a bit more dramatic—"

A light sound chimed in the galley, indicating that someone had pressed the service button. I used it as my cue to walk away from Alex and her uncomfortable statements for a minute.

Would my sexual life be more exciting with more drama?

4:05 A.M.

"ANYWAY," I continued when I returned to the galley at the back of the plane a few minutes later. "I'm over him now. Well... I'm trying to be. I realize he wasn't right for me. We ended it when he drove me to the airport."

"Way to go, that's my girl," Alex told me with a smile. "You can't end up with a cheating bastard if you never commit, and you can't be hurt by someone who doesn't belong to you. At least, that's my take on relationships."

I let her words marinate for a few minutes. She and I certainly viewed things differently... Not that she was right or wrong.

"And to think I was considering leaving my job to spend more time with him," I said.

"Whoa. Hold your horses. Men who expect women like us to give up traveling to exotic destinations... Men who want us to stop meeting new people from all over the world... They're simply not for us! You know that, right?"

Alex shook her head at me, probably recollecting a similar conversation we'd had a few months ago. She didn't share my love ideals and definitely didn't believe in 'finding the one.'

Can she be right? Have romantic movies ruined me? Are my expectations unrealistic?

I let my eyes stare into nothingness for a while, trying to forget about the whole thing.

When reality kicked back in, Alex was looking at herself in her powder case, fixing her makeup before spilling out more of her wise pearls.

"If you stop expecting things from men—or from anyone for that matter—you'll be a lot happier." She smacked her bright red lips before continuing. "For example: I don't seek relationships; I only want to find my next fling with a handsome man who can make me come like the princess that I am. Just let yourself be. Enjoy the physical company of another human being for once! One-night stands are so liberating. You should really give them a try sometime."

"Don't you have a new boyfriend? That black guy from Seattle?" I asked.

"A boyfriend? That's... way more than a stretch. But I guess I could call him a multiple-night stand. I'm seeing him again tomorrow..." She looked at her watch. "Or tonight, I should say. It'll be his first time in Toronto. Doubt he'll see more than the four walls of my hotel room, though."

I smiled at Alex.

Should I take cues from her? Should I stop caring so much about trying to find men who displayed decent relationship potential?

What I'm doing is certainly not working.

What harm is there in trying something new?

I decided to find out.

"Any tips on how to become more like you?" I asked her.

"Listen. You follow my lead and I gua-ran-tee you'll have a guy sharing that hotel room with you tonight. You up for it?"

What? Now? Here?

A wave of fear came over me.

Definitely out of my comfort zone. But then again, why not?

I raised my shoulders and nodded silently, trying to hide the fact that my heart was beating way too fast.

"That's my girl," she said before taking off her uniform jacket. "Is it just me or is it hot in here tonight?"

I nodded again. The plane *was* really warm right now, probably because whoever had set the temperature knew we didn't have enough blankets onboard for everyone.

"I've got an idea," she said before unbuttoning her shirt a little. "Seriously, follow my lead. We'll offer the passengers who are still awake an extra snack and drink service. Watch and learn."

She reached behind her back and undid her strapless bra, then pulled it out of her shirt from the front. After tucking it in the inner pocket of the jacket she'd just hung in the storage area, she pinched her nipples until they became firm and started poking through the fabric of her white shirt.

"Your turn," Alex said. I hesitated for a second and she tried to reassure me. "Hardly anyone's awake! What are you afraid of?"

Turning around to peek at the passengers, I saw that most of them were deep asleep, just like she'd said. I took off my jacket, but my bra wasn't strapless. I stepped in the bathroom for a second to take my top and bra off, then I put my long-sleeve shirt back on.

"You've got nice tits!" she said, grabbing them with both hands through the fabric of my shirt.

I was a little surprised by her lack of boundaries, but hey... I obviously needed to be more audacious.

"Let's go down the aisle. There's a cutie near the front who's still awake," she said.

We got the cart ready and I followed her, pushing our collection of overpriced airline snacks and drinks.

After picking up various pillows and items that littered our path, we finally made it to the front. Alex was all smiles, her partly unbuttoned shirt gaining the attention of Cutie-Blondie. He looked like he was around twenty-five or twenty-six years old.

"Would you like a beverage, sir?" she asked, her hand stroking her collarbone and pulling her shirt open more, allowing her forearm to push her loose breasts against each other.

"Hmm, sure. Coke?" the man asked.

"Let me see if I have any left," Alex said, maintaining eye contact with him for a couple of seconds, then bending down and letting him peer into her shirt while she was retrieving a can from the drawer. A Coca-Cola in hand, she stood back up and then popped open the can before talking to him some more. "It's so hot in here tonight," she said, moving her shirt to supposedly let some air in, but obviously letting him see more of her. "Would you like some ice with that?"

The man stirred in his seat, closed the magazine he was reading, and placed it in his lap before nodding.

Alex poured his drink slowly over a few ice cubes in a plastic cup. "Anything else?" she asked.

"Hmmm," was all Cutie-Blondie said.

"I'll be back later if you need anything."

She nodded at me, and I pulled the cart back.

We offered a quick, non-flirty service to another couple of passengers who were awake near the middle of the plane.

"Can't believe what you did," I whispered. "So smooth!"

"Now's your turn," she said. "Behind you on your left," she continued while pushing the cart.

I finally understood who she meant when I saw a brown-haired man with a pronounced 5 o'clock shadow. He was sitting alone in the second-last row, wearing jeans and a light-blue shirt. A sitcom was airing on his monitor, but he was watching us, a twinkle in his eyes.

From his aisle seat, did he see Alex's little game?

"Good evening, sir," I greeted him, flashing my biggest smile and rubbing the back of my neck, giving myself a chance to push out my breasts without being too obvious about it. I saw his eyes divert that way for a second before meeting mine.

He had a large grin on his face. "Good evening," he said.

"May I interest you in a drink?"

"Don't know. Kind of late for coffee," he said, still smiling at me.

"Well, we also have soda, beer, hard liquor, and wine. Alcohol prices are listed here," I said, grabbing a brochure and leaning way closer than necessary to offer him the pamphlet. I swear I heard him take a whiff of my scent. *Good sign?*

He took the onboard menu and inspected the listed offerings. "It's hot in here; maybe I'll have a beer, but only if it's cold," he said.

I bent down to reach into the drawer where we kept the cans. I made sure to pick the coldest beer I could find, then brought it to my cleavage, letting the chilled aluminum exterior cool me off for a second, enjoying its refreshing effect, and smiling at him.

"Yes, definitely cold," I finally replied.

He motioned for me to lean in, and I did.

"Two tips are telling me you're not lying," he whispered before brushing one of my nipples with the back of his hand.

A shiver ran down my spine.

"I'm John by the way," he said, now in a normal tone, as I returned to my cart. He handed me the brochure back, and I turned to face Alex for a second.

She winked at me, then nodded toward Cutie-Blondie and walked away, leaving me alone with John.

"Nice to meet you, John," I said.

"You accept credit cards, right?" he asked, his brown eyes meeting mine.

I smiled and nodded.

He undid his seat belt before digging in his back pocket for his wallet. While he was doing that, I grabbed the payment machine and had it ready by the time he handed me his card.

I dealt with the transaction with half my attention on him and the other automatically processing the purchase, something I could do in my sleep. I returned his card along with a printed receipt before popping open the can for him. "Glass?"

"Yes, please," he said, once again smiling at me, a devious expression in his eyes.

I poured some of the beer into the cup, then handed him the plastic container and the half-empty aluminum can. "Enjoy!" I said before pulling the cart back to its storage location.

Alex stepped into the galley a minute later.

"So?" she asked.

Is it going well? Probably.

I answered with just a smile.

"Wait for it. There's a part two," she said before glancing at the passengers and ensuring no one was looking back toward us. She rode her skirt up, pulled down her lacy white panties, and then placed them in one of the duty-free magazines that were stored in the nearby wall holder. "Here's something he can't resist." She smoothed down her skirt and walked down the aisle toward Cutie-Blondie, her loaded magazine in hand.

I stayed back and watched from a distance.

A few steps later, she leaned forward, offering him once again a good view of her cleavage. She said something, winked at him, and then handed him the magazine before coming back toward me, beaming.

"What did you tell him?"

"There's a special offer on page 24," she said, once again flashing me her white teeth. "Okay, now's your turn, lady. Handsome brown-haired guy's looking at us right now."

John was making the 'come-here' motion with his fingers, so I walked up to him.

"Sorry to bother you," he said without a word more.

"Not at all." I smiled.

He motioned for me to lean forward again. "What magazine did your colleague hand the man up front?" he asked.

"A copy of our duty-free magazine."

"I believe I might also be interested in that special offer you ladies appear to have at the moment..." His fingers, which had previously been positioned on the armrest, now grazed the side of my leg. I could feel blood rushing to my cheeks.

Jeez, he overheard that?

"Any chance you could hand me your copy of the magazine?" I didn't know what to say to that. I moved my shirt a little, not trying to expose myself, but honestly trying to ventilate so I could think more clearly.

Is it just hot or is he having an effect on me? Or both?

"Hey," he said before undoing his seat belt and moving over to the empty seat next to him. He tapped on the cushioned chair he'd occupied only a second ago. "Sit for a second."

I looked back at Alex, who'd been watching me from the nearby galley. She nodded.

Why not?

I sat next to him, and he reached up to turn on the air and direct it at me, right at my décolletage. The cooler air felt really nice. I moved my shirt to let more air in.

"So, what do you think?" he prompted again, his fingers still discreetly moving up my side. "Looks like you're feeling cooler now." The back of his hand barely touched my left breast as he spoke. My nipples were hard.

I turned to face him. He was obviously intent on getting his request fulfilled.

"So, those duty-free specials?" he asked again.

I took a deep breath and mustered all the courage I had before looking into his brown eyes and divulging the truth in a quiet whisper, "You're quite the looker... I'd love to share those specials with you... but it's just that..."

"What? Are you too shy now?" he asked, his hand now grabbing my knee firmly enough to double my heartbeat.

I licked my lips before leaning in to whisper in his ear, "No, it's just that I'm not wearing panties right now."

Yeah, stupid me.

In my rush to end things with Self-Centered-Sam, I had left behind some of my clothes, including all my panties, except for the pair I'd had on, which reeked of campfire smoke. I'd stowed them away, sealing its stench in a plastic bag in my carry-on luggage.

His eyes brightened up and he tilted his head. "Is that so? Now, that's surprising."

He now looked at me with a provocative gaze, then he leaned closer and whispered in my ear, "Any chance you could give me a quick glance?"

After asking me, he leaned back into his seat, his eyes glued on mine with the expression of the cat who'd gotten the cream. He looked around before continuing. "Not right here, of course. But if you were to grab me a snack from that bottom drawer... over there," he said, pointing to the far corner of the galley. "I'd really appreciate it."

What he'd requested was definitely not in my nature, but my competitive spirit had been challenged. By him and by Alex. "And what would I get in exchange?" I asked.

"And look who's talking now!" He eyed me up and down and leaned closer to me again, his lips a mere inch from my left ear. "Show me yours, and I'll show you mine."

I got up, stared him down, and then nodded. "Deal."

I headed to the corner of the galley, where no one but John could glance at me. Alex was nowhere to be seen, but a quick look forward confirmed she'd taken a seat next to Cutie-Blondie.

I teasingly raised the hem of my skirt, a little bit at a time, until the lacy top of my black self-adhesive stockings became visible.

John sent me a smile of approval.

I hiked my skirt up some more, front and back, until it reached the perfect height, then turned around, bent down at the hip, and then opened up one of the drawers where we kept the extra cookies and napkins. I shook my bootie a little, raising my tailbone as high as I could and spreading my legs for just a second, then turned around and lowered my skirt again.

When I looked at John, his mouth was agape. Then he joined his hands repeatedly in a silent clap.

I walked back toward him and handed the cookies and napkin I'd just got. I was about to sit down next to him when another passenger across the aisle saw the offering and requested cookies as well.

"Of course, just a second," I said to the man, feeling my cheeks redden as I walked away.

When I reached the galley, I turned around, John was looking at me, a large smirk on his face, his eyebrows raised.

Is he expecting a second show?

I shook my head. Playtime was over. More and more passengers were waking up, so I put on my jacket, hiding my unsupported breasts for now until I could put my bra back on later.

Now looking—and acting—more professional, I brought the requested treat to the other passenger then discreetly addressed my flirty brown-haired man. "And I believe you owe me something, Mr. John."

"Of course," he said before getting up and

taking his phone into the unoccupied washroom next to the galley.

In the mean time, Alex returned to the back, put on her jacket, and we both started getting ready for the final drink service.

"So, how's it going with 48C?" she asked.

"I think you'd be proud of me."

She leaned in, brimming. "Tell me more!"

"Later—he's in the washroom," I whispered, pointing at the door a mere two feet away from us.

"Ooh la la, can't wait."

I DIDN'T SEE my handsome John come out of the lavatory until the final service had started.

By the time I reached his row at the back of the plane, he'd returned to his assigned seat. He had his phone ready, as if paying in kind for the abysmal cup of coffee I was about to pour for him.

"It's unlocked. Just look at the last photo," he said, handing me the device. I took it, placed it in my jacket pocket, and then finished serving the other seats across the aisle before pushing the cart away, finally able to view my reward.

"Wow!" I couldn't help but gasp when I saw his large cock on the screen. Alex came over, and I hid the phone, but John was looking at me and had seen me react. By the way his shoulders lifted, I understood he didn't care whether or not the image was kept private. I showed Alex the photo and she smiled, sending flirty eyes toward John. A polite nod later, he turned his gaze toward me. I mimicked his previous silent clapping motion.

John got up from his seat and walked toward me. Alex stepped away and headed to help a passenger who'd just pressed the assistance button.

What now? This was brand new territory for me, so I didn't know what to expect.

I extended the hand with which I was holding his phone. He was probably coming here to get it back.

"It's a little late for me to suggest we join a certain club, but maybe we could... grab a coffee when this plane lands? What do you think?" he asked.

Alex's previous remarks about my need to have a one-night stand still echoed in my mind. "Why not?" I finally replied.

He scribbled his number on the corner of a nearby in-flight magazine and ripped it off before handing it to me.

"Call me, gorgeous! I'll be in Toronto for a few days."

"Maybe," was all I said, and he returned to his seat just as the captain turned on the seat belt sign and announced that we'd be landing shortly.

7:00 P.M.

I DONNED a classy yet simple black skirt with a silky white blouse and slipped on my new heels over the Band-Aid covered blisters I'd gotten earlier in the day.

After taking one last look in the mirror, I spritzed a dash of jasmine on my neck and left my room to head to the place that Alex had recommended.

Once seated in the contemporary-fusion restaurant, I ordered myself a steak and french fries with a glass of Bordeaux. Meeting her down here was somewhat unlikely—with her quasi-boyfriend being in town tonight—but who knew. Maybe I'd find a kind soul to converse with over a drink.

The short, curly-haired bartender was cute. I smiled at him, but he showed no interest in me. A handsome man came and sat a few bar stools away from me. My efforts to make eye contact with him proved futile.

Fifteen minutes of light background jazz music later, a short brunette joined him. His wife. Good for him.

Fed, alone, lonely, and without any sign of Alex —she was probably getting laid now—I returned to my hotel room, anxious to watch a movie or do something to once again get my mind off Self-Centered-Sam and his cheating ways.

Why am I still thinking about him?

I was toying with the idea of calling John but somehow couldn't bring myself to do it. Was it too romantic of me to want something more than a one-night stand with a stranger? Even a good-looking one with a nice cock?

After unlocking my door with the magnetic card, I flipped on the lights and kicked my heels off. It was incredibly hot in my room. I walked over to the air conditioning unit by the window.

Just as I was about to cut off what was left of daylight outside and block out the bright lampposts that already illuminated the inside courtyard of my hotel—yes, I had a crappy view of other people's suites—I found the perfect distraction for me. It was exactly what I needed this very minute: a naked couple going at it two floors down, across the courtyard from me.

Their lights were on, their blinds wide open. It was an open invitation for all voyeurs out there, and I was certainly one of them. However, not being of the exhibitionist variety, I decided to turn off my lights before sliding the large padded chair directly in front of the window, where I could get a good view of the action without being seen. It was like watching my neighbor's porn channel through my bedroom curtains. I couldn't make out their exact facial expressions or even their traits, but sometimes these things were best left to the imagination.

A tall and slender woman was on all fours, naked on the bed, her head facing the headboard, ankles and feet dangling off the end of the mattress. Her red hair draped and hid her face. Behind her, a black, muscular man was doing her doggy style. His large hands contrasted against her ivory body, like two huge ink spots. Her breasts bounced forward and back, almost hitting her in the face. The visual intrusion on their actions felt so real and close, I could almost hear the flapping noises of their skin.

She put her face down on the comforter, resting her breasts against the bed and lifting her ass to change the man's penetration angle.

I couldn't resist. My view would be so much more entertaining and enjoyable as an interactive experience. To add to that, the various scenarios my mind had imagined since my encounter with John hadn't done anything to suppress my horniness.

Without hesitation, I stood up and took off my skirt and the new panties I'd bought to replace the pairs I'd left behind, then sat back down, resting my feet on the air conditioning unit in front of me. I adjusted the knobs to the coolest setting and let the powerful breeze tease my trimmed pussy. I undid the top three buttons of my shirt and slid one hand into my bra to get a hold of one of my breasts. The other hand joined the breeze in caressing my exposed lips.

Just as I got comfortable, the couple changed position. The woman pulled away from the man and stood up before walking toward the window. The man followed. He stood about a foot taller than her. As they passed the writing desk, he grabbed her by the hips and sat her down on the solid piece of furniture.

Wonderful. Perfect viewing point.

They were probably a foot from the window, the entire desk visible and their beautiful bodies exposed for the world—or at least the whole courtyard—to see.

He pulled up her legs one at a time and rested them against his strong shoulders, then his black shaft entered her. He slid her toward him, letting her head and back rest on the desk while he held her ass in his large hands, banging her with ardor.

I inserted a finger inside me, then two, imagining his large black cock fucking me. I matched my rhythm to his, my other hand caressing my breasts, then moving down to my clit.

The woman lifted her arms up, and he slowed down. She reached up to wrap her arms around his neck. While still inside her, he lifted her from the desk and pressed her back and ass against the window. Each of his pushes flattened the woman's exposed bottom and lifted her up slightly.

I finger-fucked myself harder, faster.

I pinched my nipples, making them erect, then returned to my clit. I couldn't help but arch my back, moving closer to the window as if the couple across from me were magnetically attracting me, supporting my orgasm, increasing my heartbeat along with theirs. My body approached the quivering point.

As the first wave of pleasure exploded from within me, I saw the man peer out the window, over his partner's shoulder, in my direction, as if he'd seen me. Then I recognized Alex. They were both looking out the window in my direction, probably in their own post-orgasmic euphoria.

But they can't see me. No, that can't be. My lights are off.

I nonetheless closed the curtains.

And who cares if they saw me.

Alex certainly wouldn't care. In fact, she'd probably be happy about it. And I'd just had a great show, free of charge, shame, and guilt. Well, mostly. I now knew what Alex's layovers were like.

Feeling a little less bored, I took a shower to cool off and return to reality. Maybe I'd find myself a hot lover like Alex had. Actually... maybe I had this lover's number in my purse.

Is it just a matter of picking up the phone and finding out?

HE PICKED up on the second ring.

"John?" I started, "It's—"

He started talking before I could introduce myself. "Hi, gorgeous. I was hoping you'd call. Do you want to meet?"

His sexy voice made what was left of my hesitation evaporate.

"Join me at Korimate?" I offered.

"Sure, I know where it is. Thirty minutes?"

I felt an irrepressible smile appear on my face. "Perfect. I'm already here, sitting at the bar."

After hanging up, I rested my phone on the marble countertop. I got the attention of the bartender. *Work shifts must have changed.* A blonde woman with her hair neatly tied up in a ponytail now manned the bar. I asked for a glass of Chardonnay.

Excitement and a little bit of apprehension entered my mind. I stared at my nails and resisted the urge to bite them and ruin my manicure. My reflection in the large mirror behind the bar guided me in readjusting how my red necklace fell into my cleavage. I still had that healthy, rosy glow that resulted from having come just a little while ago.

I told myself that I looked okay, as attractive as I could be with what nature had granted me. I was staring at the bottom of my empty wine glass when I heard John's sexy voice behind me.

"Hey, there!" he said, placing his hand on my waist and kissing me on the left cheek, but ever so close to my lips. I inhaled his cologne. *Aqua Blue?* I once dated a guy who wore that delicious scent all the time. Before I could go down memory lane and remember who that was, he started talking.

"What's your poison?" he asked, noticing the empty glass in front of me.

"Cave Spring Estate Bottled Chardonnay Musqué," I replied.

He got the bartender's attention and ordered our drinks while I took the opportunity to have a good look at him. I had found him quite handsome on the plane, but now he was quite simply a tall, dark, and handsome stud in his jeans and crisp white shirt.

How I loved men with cufflinks... *Fairly wealthy?*

A few minutes later, drinks in hand, we headed toward an empty booth near the back of the bar.

"You've kept me waiting a long time," he said after we sat down next to each other on the crescent-shaped red leather seat. "But I'm really glad you called."

"Well—"

"And I really have to consider making your airline my preferred choice if that's how you ladies serve your passengers," he continued, sliding his finger along my lower arm.

I felt my cheeks redden. "That's not regular service," I said, smiling. "Doubt you'll have the same experience again on one of our flights."

"That's too bad, but I'm glad I did."

He slid closer to me in the booth.

"So where did we leave off?" he asked, one of his arms wrapped around my shoulders while the other slid down to my leg.

"About there, I guess." I had goose bumps and could feel myself getting wet already. Half of me couldn't believe I was actually capable of meeting a quasi-stranger in a bar, going through with a one-night stand. But my body was clearly fine with the idea. I ordered my mind to shut up and just enjoy it.

"Are you still lacking a certain piece of clothing?" he asked with a crooked smile.

I thought about how much I had stressed out earlier about whether or not to wear my new panties for him. "Actually, I had a chance to go shopping this afternoon... But I left those in my hotel room."

"I don't believe you. Mind if I check?"

His fingers moved to outline the hem of my skirt, which sat about four inches below my pussy. I looked down, the table wasn't draped with a tablecloth, but the lights were low. Chances were that none of the people in the bar would notice anything. I parted my legs slightly in agreement.

His digits slid up my inner thighs and stopped just short for a second, his eyes locked onto mine. My slight annoyance at his stopping must have shown on my face because his smile became a little more crooked when he resumed and finally reached my pussy.

At first, his fingertips just tickled me. But I wanted more.

I lowered myself to get closer to his hand by an inch or two, hiking my skirt in the process. He leaned in to brush his lips against my neck. His kisses were ocean-scented whispers that only served to crank up my horniness. But his fingers were more eager. His thumb teased my clit while the tip of two of his fingers circled my pussy, pinched my lips, then finally entered me just a tad.

His mouth met mine in a fervent kiss. Our tongues intertwined, his passion apparently as high as mine. His hand was still busy with my pussy, but he pulled his mouth away from my lips and moved on to kiss my ear.

"You're so wet. I love it," he whispered before nibbling on my earlobe.

Two of his fingers were now fully inside me, and I swear I could hear how lubricated my pussy was. I wanted him. I couldn't wait any longer.

"I want you to fuck me," I whispered in his ear.

"Right here in this booth?" he asked, pulling away from me, a big smirk on his face.

By now, all I could think of was finding the closest private—or semi-private—location. My hotel room was way too far. I wanted him this minute.

A quick glance around provided the answer I needed.

"The bathroom. Join me in the ladies' in thirty seconds," I ordered while grabbing a napkin from the table, pushing his hand out of the way, and then quickly wiping my inner legs. I awkwardly pulled down on my skirt just as I exited the booth.

After grabbing my purse, I headed to the washroom.

On my way there, I saw my reflection in the mirror behind the bar: my cheeks were red—blame it on the wine or him?—and my hair was a little out of place. I drew my hand through it to smooth it out a bit. I was so turned on by John that I could almost feel my heartbeat in my genitals.

A few steps later, I turned into a hallway and pushed open the door to the ladies' room. A fifty-something woman stood in front of the mirror reapplying lipstick.

Damn. Is she almost done? Staying?

Unsure, I washed my hands in the sink next to hers. We shared a silent smile across the mirror; then she headed into a stall.

Shit!

I quickly dried my hands and then walked out just as John arrived at the door.

"Occupied," I said discreetly, then I noticed the large handicapped bathroom a few steps away. I nodded in that direction, and we both headed that way.

A few seconds later, we arrived at the large door. He checked it, and it opened right away.

"Ladies first," he gallantly offered. I snuck in and he joined me in the industrial-cleaner-scented room before locking the door behind us.

I made my way to the sink and rested my small black, silky handbag against the mirror. My heart pounded in my chest.

Am I really going to go through with this? Can I be that kind of woman?

His voice brought me back to the here and now.

"A bit larger than an airplane's washroom, but it still works for me," he said, moving toward me before framing my head in his hands, and then kissing me.

I backed up until my back hit the tiled wall partition that separated the toilet from the sink area. He lifted me up and sat me next to the low, wheelchair-accessible wash basin. He unbuttoned my blouse, digging in to expose my bra and feel my breasts. After helping me get the blouse off, his hands reached behind my back and released my breasts from their lacy prison. I pulled my arms out of the bra straps and tossed my undergarment to join my blouse in the sink next to me.

"Ah, those gorgeous tits!" he said, moving away from me slightly as if wanting to take in the view. "You know you were driving me mad, the way you were moving that beer can in your cleavage on the plane? I just wanted to suck on your tits, squeeze them, pinch those nipples."

I could feel my cheeks flush.

Being so blatantly seen as the object of a hot guy's sexual desires was a first for me. Cloud nine—or maybe nine hundred—was my emotional address at that exact moment.

John neared me again and began massaging my breasts. I reached for his silver belt buckle and unfastened it. He wore button-up jeans, and I undid the metal fasteners one at a time, very aware of his erect cock ready to pop out. Halfway done, I squeezed one hand into his jeans and grabbed his firm ass, pleasantly surprised to realize he was commando. I undid the last few buttons and finally exposed his glorious cock. I brought him closer to me and kissed him.

Our mouths were hungry, demanding, but my pussy was the horniest of all. Two of his fingers fucked me while I stroked him with my hand. I pulled out of his embrace for a second to reach into my purse for a condom.

He used this opportunity to go down on me. Spreading my legs wider and licking my inner thighs, then the tip of his tongue teased my lips, my clit... I pulsated with desire. I needed to have his hard cock in me now.

I tore open the condom wrapper. "I like what you're doing, but I want you to fuck me. Now."

He came back up, kissed me, and I unrolled the ultra-thin latex on his glorious cock.

The counter was not suitable for intercourse with me sitting by the sink: he was tall and the counter was ridiculously low for that purpose. He lifted me up, my skirt now hiked to my waist, and then pushed me against the cold tiled wall in the corner. I didn't care. I just wanted him inside of me. Now.

His eyes locked on mine; the tip of his cock penetrated me. I let out a sigh. I felt my insides parting to make way for his glorious appendage.

Finally!

I wrapped my legs around his ass and my arms

around his neck and back. He started to fuck me, hard. He was grunting quietly, and I tried to keep quiet although my instincts were to moan. I almost lost my breath as my heartbeat kept increasing.

"Fuck me harder!" I whispered in his ear.

"I want to take you from behind," he said, pulling out of me.

I unwrapped my legs and put them down. He held me up for a second as I got on my feet, feeling a little uneasy on my heels.

My blood must have concentrated in my pussy.

A couple of seconds later, having regained my balance, I moved to face the mirror, with him standing behind me. He grabbed one of my exposed breasts in his hand and looked at our reflection above the sink: him standing behind me, kissing my neck, my skirt bunched up at my waist, my pussy and tits exposed, wanting his attention. With my heels on, it looked as though I was the perfect height for him to take me from behind.

His lips left my neck, and he bent me forward. I leaned to rest my hands against the low counter. He thrust his cock in my pussy again, and his hands grabbed a hold of my hips. John started pounding into me, my breasts bouncing with each push. I let go of the counter and reached to grab a hold of them. I pinched my nipples and locked eyes with him through the mirror as he penetrated me, over and over. His eyes then looked down toward his cock.

For a second, I wished I'd taken off his shirt earlier. I could only imagine how chiseled his abs would be. I released one of my breasts and brought my hand to my clit to rub it.

"You like it?" he asked, his eyes once again meeting mine through the mirror.

"Hell, yeah! Fuck me, John." I arched my back, enjoying the new angle his cock took inside of me. It was now hitting me exactly where I wanted it. I felt my legs getting weak. A first wave of tremors took me over, and he pounded me harder, deeper. I bit my lips, then sighed. I couldn't help but quiver. A second wave flooded over me when he gave me his final push, accompanied by an animal grunt.

"Fuck, yeah," he finally said, folding his body over mine. "You're everything I imagined you'd be," he whispered in my ear.

"And so are you," I said. "And more," I continued after I felt him pull his cock out.

I turned around to face the gorgeous man who'd just made me come. John was holding the condom with one hand, carefully keeping its contents inside. He was biting his lips. For a second, I wondered what life with him would be like; but then I realized I didn't know anything about John, and that was probably better.

I felt my own juices running down my legs and reached for a paper towel. He grabbed my breasts again and kissed them.

A knock on the locked door followed by a brisk attempt at opening it terminated the moment.

"Occupied," John said aloud. "Give me a few more minutes."

I grabbed my bra and put it back on. I lowered my skirt, donned my blouse, and then fixed my hair.

"Wanna go out first?" he asked in a whisper.

There was no way we'd be able to leave this room discreetly. I raised my shoulders.

What would be less embarrassing?

"Don't know," I said, finally.

"You go first. I'll deal with whoever it is."

After grabbing my purse and giving a final glance at my reflection to make sure all of my clothes were back on and I hadn't left anything behind, I kissed him.

"Thanks for calling me. Maybe we can do that again?" he offered after ending our kiss.

I walked away from him and crossed the short

distance that separated me from the door. He stayed back, leaning against the sink.

"Maybe," I said before blowing him a kiss and unlocking the door.

As I exited into the hallway, the frowning face of the blonde ponytailed bartender greeted me. I shot her a fake smile and walked away as fast as my heels would let me, mortification adding to my already orgasmically blushed cheeks.

I walked out of the bar and headed back to my hotel room.

ALONE, lying in the comfortable queen-sized hotel bed, just as I was about to set the alarm on my phone, a flashback of John's brown eyes and fantastic cock came to mind.

A wave of something went through my body, and I felt my cheeks flush for the umpteenth time today.

Is it delight? Embarrassment? Excitement? Shame? A sexual craving for more?

How can my actions over the past few hours feel so wrong yet so right at the same time?

Getting out of my head for a second, I flipped through my phone contacts until I came across the one labeled 'Toronto John.'

I stared at it for a second.

Could be nice to see him again... He could be my Toronto fling. Maybe more?

Damn it! Why can't I turn this relationship-seeking instinct off?

I hit the 'delete' button before I could talk myself into keeping his number.

I'll never know what his last name is and it doesn't matter. I'll always have the memory of meeting Toronto John on that flight and sharing one special experience with him.

Alex's probably right.

Could I enjoy men without feeling the need to have a relationship with them?

Maybe.

Hmmm. I think a new and much more exciting phase of my life has just begun.

PART TWO

MY XXX EXPERIENCE

THE PLAN

MY MYSTERY STEWARDESS left me three options:

OPTION 1: Canvass all airlines that fly into Toronto, Canada, and find a red-headed flight attendant named Alex who could potentially identify my mystery stewardess.

I'm a positive guy and I like a good challenge, but considering that at least sixty-five airlines fly into YYZ/Pearson, and that each has a drove of flight attendants (not to mention high personnel turn-over)... I don't have enough contacts in high places to pull the right strings to get all the confidential information I'd need.

Likelihood of success: Close to nil.

OPTION 2: Go to the campground near Banff and potentially run into the employee who could then lead me to the stewardess's ex-boyfriend, who could direct me to her.

At least I have the campground's name. The rest would depend on luck. Small campgrounds can't have that many employees, right? Worst case, I could stay there a few extra days or kindly ask whoever is working at the time to get the right employee's phone number. Would her ex have kept her contact information? Possibly.

Likelihood of success: Average.

OPTION 3: Find Toronto John.

I don't even think that guy lives in Toronto. And even if I were to randomly bump into the right brown-haired, brown-eyed man named John out of sheer luck, I don't think she gave him her details. Does he even know her name? But then again, maybe the blonde ponytailed waitress could be bribed into looking at old credit card receipts? But I have no idea *when* the stewardess was in that restaurant/bar... Last month? Last year? Five years ago?

Likelihood of success: Sliver of hope.

The campground/ex-boyfriend route is definitely the best plan of attack.

WHAT HAPPENED

AFTER A FEW WELL-PLACED CALLS, I managed to locate the campground the stewardess had mentioned in her journal. Wasn't easy, but an old colleague who'd turned bush pilot had access to detailed cartographic maps of southern British Columbia and Alberta, and he pinpointed it for me.

Taking advantage of a few scheduled days off, I flew to nearby YYC/Calgary airport on a Tuesday morning with a small carry-on bag full of outdoor clothes. I then rented an SUV and made my way to a sports rental store to find the camping gear I'd need.

Another short trip followed, this time to the

grocery store to fill my cooler with ice, beer, and camping food, and then I was good to go.

Here's how it went down.

11:30 A.M.

THE SLANTED PINE Roads campground was located in an idyllic sequestered spot in the large pine forests of the Rocky Mountains, quite a few miles from the Trans-Canada Highway.

After veering off onto a dirt road, I drove about a mile before passing under a carved wooden sign welcoming me to the site. I immediately spotted the reception building and parked my rental vehicle in front of the small rustic shack.

I turned off the ignition and stepped out, inhaling the fresh air. What real pine-scent was like.

Refreshing.

I walked into the reception area that obviously doubled as a small camping supply store. Piles of firewood for sale were stacked on the left side of the door, and a large electric ice cooler occupied the other side. After walking up a couple of steps, I opened the squeaky door and entered, triggering a bell in the process.

Inside the building, behind a small counter, a freckled twenty-something girl with frizzy reddish-blonde hair and a hunter-like red and black plaid flannel shirt was seated on a stool, book in hand. But the bell had made her look up toward me, and she greeted me with a smile.

"Hi there," I said, wondering if she was the one who'd gotten frisky with the ex-boyfriend.

"Hey!" she replied, placing her Harlequin romance down on the counter and jumping to her feet.

"Do you have a spot available for tonight?"

"Of course," she said before walking around the counter to join me on the customer side.

I couldn't help but notice how large her boobs were for her petite frame. They brought her shirt up in the front, exposing a little bit of jean fabric past the flaps of her flannel shirt. Otherwise, her barely tanned legs were exposed all the way down to her rolled gray wool socks and brown leather hiking boots.

The barely visible skirt, the socks, the boots... She has to be the woman the stewardess described in her journal.

I decided to ask the campground employee what I had come here to find out.

"This is going to sound a little strange, but I'm trying to find a friend of a friend who comes camping here," I said.

She tilted her head and stared at me with a strange look in her eyes, her eyebrows angled. "I'm not sure I can be much help. Lots of people come here."

"His name's Sam."

"Sam who?"

"That, I don't know."

A few seconds went by. She turned her palms up. "You'll have to give me a little bit more than that."

"He's Canadian. You may have gone to school with him."

"How would you know that?" she asked, but I remained silent, hopeful that she'd still answer my out-of-the-left-field question. Her eyes veered toward the top left corner, *accessing her memory bank?* "Most people who know about this campground are Canadians. For some reason, we've never quite made the official campground maps. And I've gone to school with a few Sams. I need a bit more."

"Okay," I leaned closer to her and put my hand on her shoulder. "I know one more detail."

She didn't seem bothered by me touching her. "Shoot," she said, a smile on her face.

I hesitated for a second, then voiced the awkward words I had been hoping I wouldn't have to say aloud, "His dick leans to the left."

Her eyes were now wide open. "What? Now, that's a detail I didn't expect! Didn't peg you as a player for the other team," she said, placing her hand flat on my six-pack abs, just above my belt.

I shook my head sharply. "I'm not gay!"

Being mistaken for a gay guy's a first. But my question certainly didn't help my case.

"Are you a cop or P.I.?" she asked.

I didn't understand what was going on in this woman's brain. "Do I look like a cop or private eye?"

"Maybe you're more of a *Privates' Inspector* then?" she asked with a wink and a smile.

Is she flirting with me?

"Well, tell you what," she said, getting back to business. "Most spots are open for tonight."

She looked out the window at my parked vehicle before addressing me again.

"Sleeping in a tent or in the back of your Cherokee?" she asked.

"Haven't decided yet. Got a tent in there."

"Well, why don't you go and set yourself up at number 12 over here," she said, circling a number on a photocopied map of the site. She marked two other icons: the bathroom and garbage area. "Don't keep any food outside of your vehicle. We had bear sightings a few days ago."

"That settles the tent question. I'll sleep in the back of my SUV!"

"As you wish," she replied in a nonchalant way, obviously not as scared of bears as I was. "So it's fifteen dollars for the night."

"Okay," I said, then took my wallet out and retrieved one purple and one blue bill. "So, do you know the Sam I'm talking about?" I asked as I handed her the exact change.

"Maybe..." she said, taking my money and then handing me the map.

"Any way you could help me track him down?"

"Depends."

"Depends on what?"

"Meet me in the bathroom in a few minutes. I'll

show you how to work the shower and I'll decide then. Maybe," she repeated, eyeing me down.

I bid my goodbye for now then turned around, my black-and-white map in hand, before stepping outside to return to my vehicle.

HAVING DRIVEN around the whole campground to reach my spot, I now knew that the place was near vacant. There was one RV parked a few sites down, but otherwise it was empty.

Guess nobody goes camping in the middle of nowhere on a Tuesday, even on a sunny day.

I backed the Cherokee to fit into the limits of my campsite, making sure it was on even ground so I could get a good night's sleep. Vehicle in place, I then made my way to the bathroom, hoping the campground attendant would be able to help me track down Sam.

It was a basic concrete-block structure painted white with green metal doors and a matching green roof, but it had electricity and running water. Everything I had imagined. Nothing more, nothing less.

"Hello?" I said aloud, wondering if the friendly young woman was already in here.

No reply. The building was empty.

I took the opportunity to empty my bladder. The wall in front of the urinals was plastered with graffiti. I let my wandering eyes read some:

"Don't ruin a good thing by divulging our little secret!"

"Some things are better kept out of guide books."

What are those making reference to?

Bladder relieved, I headed to the other side of the room to wash my hands. I was admiring my two-day beard in the mirror, trying to see if any grays had started to appear among my light-brown stubble, when the employee burst into the men's room.

"Good. You found the place," she said, a big smile on her face.

I looked at her again, pretty certain that she'd unbuttoned her shirt some more since I'd last seen her. I could now see her cleavage line. A couple of fleshy, natural-looking breasts sat under there.

"Hard to miss. There aren't that many buildings around here," I replied.

"Well, that's the way we like it here, mister."

"Call me Charlie," I said, walking to her to shake her hand.

"I'm Tiffany." She shook my hand briefly then took an impromptu seat on the counter next to the sink, just a few inches from me. Her skirt barely reached the fold of her hips. Her legs were spread apart ever so slightly. I was willing to bet that if I stepped back by a few feet, with a furtive glance, I'd be able to see her panties. But before I could move, she started talking again.

"About the shower. See that machine next to the knob?" she asked, pointing at the wall in front of her.

Perfect opportunity for me to change my point of view.

I turned and took five steps toward it, then pivoted once more to look at her again.

Before making eye contact, I took a peek at her groin.

No panties? Is she aware I can totally see her bush?

I looked up, and a large grin adorned her face.

"It works with loonies. Do you have any?" she

asked as she spread her legs open some more. However, she immediately rested both of her palms in between, blocking my view of her pussy but leaning forward and framing her boobs between her arms and making her cleavage crevice more inviting than ever.

I cleared my throat and shook my head. "Your dollar coins? No. Don't have any," I answered.

"If you're interested in giving me a hand, I can show you how to get three minutes of hot water for free."

A hand?

A little confused by her request and exhibitionism, I raised my shoulders. I needed to get the information I came here to get. "And what about Sam? Can you tell me something about him?"

"Well..." she started before pausing. Her hands went to the topmost button that was still done up on her plaid shirt. She slowly undid it, then repeated the process with every button while staring at me with her green eyes.

The last one undone, she took her flannel layer off, and then threw it on the floor. Surprisingly, under her lumberjack shirt, she had on a beautiful black laced bra. She pulled one of her huge breasts out of its classy cup, pushing down the unexpectedly stretchy fabric, and then repeated with the other before caressing their curves and squeezing them together.

"So the Sam you were asking about earlier..." she said, continuing to give me a show while getting my brain's attention back to why I was here in the first place.

"Yeah?"

She remained quiet, eyeing me up and down.

I stood still and silent, save for my eyes—they were busy taking in her performance. Increased blood flow rushed below my belt, causing a bulge in my jeans.

"Thing is, I have a lot in common with him," she continued. "Some people say our libido is just too high. I say these folks can't appreciate a good thing when they have it in front of them."

And with those last words, she parted her legs even more before bringing one of her feet to the edge of the counter. Her pussy was now fully displayed. Below the bushy mat, her fingers parted her thick pink lips. I could hear how wet she was from where I stood. She fingered herself, then brought the guilty digit to her lips and licked it.

"I've got needs. Some call me a nympho. Some

call me a slut. As long as they give me the attention I want, as long as they fuck me, I don't care what label I get." She returned her hand to her pussy, while the other toyed with one of her huge breasts. "You need a written invitation?" she asked.

Still stunned by her behavior and revelation, I was unsure if the annoyed tone of her voice was for real or not, but it didn't matter. No living-and-breathing man would let an opportunity like that slip by.

I moved toward her, my hands instantly going for her tits. I kneaded her natural, fleshy mounds for a few delicious seconds. Squeezing them, I appreciated what talents Mother Nature had granted her. My hands were nowhere big enough to grab all of their plump goodness. My cock pushed hard against the fabric of my jeans, indicating its desire to participate sooner rather than later. I was about to bend down to kiss her nipples when she reached for my belt and started undoing it. "No, wait," I hesitated before continuing.

With that kind of sexual history, I should probably take precautions.

"I don't have condoms on me. They're in my vehicle," I said.

She stopped me before I could move away by

tugging on my collar. She then nodded toward a wall dispenser a few feet away from us.

"No need to put money in it. Just pop the side latch," she whispered in my ear. "So, what's it going to be, Mr. Charlie? Can you give me a hand or not?"

I couldn't think or talk.

All of my blood—and common sense—had already left my mind and reached my groin. I let her finish undoing my belt, then the zipper of my jeans. With her expert hands, she reached into my underwear and let my engorged member out for air before lowering my boxer briefs and jeans and letting them fall around my ankles.

Finally comfortable.

"Well, look at what we've got here," she said, a luscious smile appearing on her pink lips. "You may be quiet, but you sure make up for it in size, shall we say?"

She jumped off of the counter and knelt in front of me, her bare knees on the concrete floor. She immediately swallowed the tip of my dick.

"Oh," I let out, feeling the warmth of her moist mouth.

She tightened her lips around my shaft, and I pulled her head closer, letting her swallow another six inches or so, but then I felt the back of her throat. Tiffany readjusted herself, and then, as if by magic, she continued to take more of my length into her mouth.

My eyes rolled back. With my hands wrapped around her frizzy hair, I increased her cadence, pulling her head toward me. I fucked her hungry mouth. Faster, faster... but then she pulled away before standing up.

"What?" I let out.

"I want you to fuck me. I want your big dick in my cunt. I need to feel you in me."

She walked toward the wall, her barely supported boobs bouncing with every step. When she reached the condom dispenser, with a flick of her fingers, she unlatched the side of the machine. She grabbed a handful of rubbers and walked back to me, placing her newly acquired goods on the counter next to us.

I unwrapped the closest wrapper and covered my cock with the thin, lubricated latex. She faced the mirror and bent forward over the counter, letting her huge breasts hang to rest against the stainless steel counter. Her mini-skirt was pulled up; her white ass and bushy pussy were winking at me, desperately waiting to be filled.

I pushed myself into her dripping, engorged opening. She was surprisingly tight considering what she'd just told me about herself. She felt goddamn awesome. Her salty and lightly musky scent filled the air.

I pounded into her, slow at first, but deep.

She moaned.

She roared.

Through the mirror, I saw her biting her lower lip. Her eyes were closed. With every one of my motions, her roars echoed in the empty building. Her outspoken behavior was turning me on a lot more than I'd expected.

"Put your finger in my ass," she ordered.

The sight of her bouncing boobs in the mirror was hypnotizing, but I obeyed. I lubricated my middle finger inside her, and then took my digit out of her pussy to circle her anus briefly before pushing my fingertip into her ass. Her roars got louder and louder.

"Faster! Deeper!" she yelled. Through the mirror, I saw one of her hands frantically rubbing her clit, then I felt her reaching for my balls.

I twisted my finger in her anus, then squeezed my index in beside it. I fucked her hard and fast while fingering her ass. Her moans had turned into howler-monkey-like noises after she'd arched her back, making herself feel even tighter. This was too much stimulation. I was about to come.

"Fuck me, Charlie. Fuck me, hard!" she ordered before I gave her my all.

A minute or so later, having caught my breath and my heartbeat now back to normal, I pulled out of her, carefully holding the semen-filled condom. I pulled up the clothes from around my ankles to my thighs so I could walk over to the garbage can and dispose of the used latex, then returned to her.

She'd already turned around and was once again sitting on the counter. I allowed my fingers to circle her large, pink areolae.

"Anything else you want to know about Sam?" she asked. Her cheeks were rosy and her eyes seemed more peaceful, as if I had somehow tamed something inside of her.

"I'm trying to find one of his ex-girlfriends," I said.

Tiffany almost choked on a giggle. "Well, good luck with that!"

"What do you mean?" I asked her, taking my hands off of her.

She reinserted her tits into her bra while replying, "He's brought many here over the years, but he stopped coming last fall. I think his wife finally found out about this place... and me, I guess. Haven't seen him since. I don't have his number anymore. He's changed it."

"Damn it."

I tucked my deflated dick back in my boxer briefs before doing up my jeans.

Well. It was worth a shot.

"But if you stick around and come see me at the front when you're bored, I may remember a few more details," she said before jumping down from the counter and stealing a kiss from me. She lowered her skirt, grabbed the flannel shirt that was laying on the concrete floor, and then walked to the shower knob.

"Crank it two full rotations clockwise and you'll get about three minutes of hot water," she said before smiling at me and heading out of the men's room in her bra, shirt in hand.

And just like that, I think I finally understood some people's fascination with camping.

9:30 P.M.

WITH A LONG SPIKE, I poked the red coals from my amateur campfire.

Although it had been years since I'd had to build a fire of any kind, my memories and experiences from the Boy Scouts decades ago came in handy.

The coals' intense heat combined with the lack of high flames would be perfect for cooking my steak now. I carefully flipped the foil-wrapped potato I'd added onto the metal grill about five minutes ago, and then threw my one-inch-thick slab of meat next to it. I didn't have any spices, but that was alright. Smoke would work just fine as a flavor-enhancer. And Alberta beef should be pretty darn good to start with.

How perfectly the day turned out!

A smile drew on my face just thinking back about the afternoon. I dug a hand in my jeans and readjusted my junk. I couldn't recall having been this raw in years. Turned out that Tiffany had no useful information for me, but she was definitely worth a fuck or two... or four. That hot—albeit hairy—Canadian pussy was insatiable.

Flannel and wool will never be the same again; they've suddenly gained a new sexual connotation. *Maybe the same goes for pine-scented objects as well?*

I flipped my meat on the grill and gulped down another swig of beer.

Stronger than our American varieties. Good stuff. Or is it the lingering pussy taste in my mouth that's affecting the flavor? Either-or.

In the distance, I saw headlights making the rounds around the site. *Must be Tiffany, checking up on things.* The headlights stopped by the RV a few sites down, then the roaring engine grew quiet and the headlights turned off.

By the time my steak felt firm (about medium doneness) and ready to eat, I heard the roar of her engine again.

Her doctor's visit to the neighbor is over?

Tiffany's headlights turned back on and headed my way; she was continuing her rounds.

I transferred my steak onto my plate and started cutting away. I was chewing on my first tasty bite when I saw her silhouette appear by the light of the fire.

"Hey, stranger," she greeted me. "Everything good?"

I smiled at her, nodding and still chewing. I stabbed another piece of meat on my fork and pointed it at her. "Want a bite?"

"Why not?" she said before taking the fork from my hand and eating my offering. "Tasty," she said after swallowing it.

"Want a beer?" I offered.

"I'm still working for another thirty minutes. Later?"

"Sure."

She nodded and turned around to return to her vehicle.

I watched her tight ass walk away from me for a few steps before the light of the fire no longer shone on her.

It's okay to fuck on the job, but she can't drink? Is that part of Canadian laws?

I smiled and shook my head before cracking open another can of beer. I leaned my head back for a minute to stare at the sky above; a shooting star crossed the sky.

I couldn't think of anything to wish for other than to find my mystery stewardess... And for the Yankees to win the World Series?

THE CRACKLING sounds of the fire had me hypnotized. Sitting on a large log, wrapped in a wool blanket, I was lost in my own thoughts. I didn't hear Tiffany's footsteps until she was right there next to me, her hand on my shoulder.

"Hey," she said. "Looks like you're ready for bed." She leaned in and kissed me. She was still wearing that same flannel shirt and the near-inexistent skirt.

"Aren't you cold?" I asked, opening my blanket and expecting her to sit on my lap. But instead, she pulled her miniskirt up—exposing her pussy as if it were a body part like any other—then opened her legs and got on mine, facing me.

After wrapping her arms around me, she locked her lips onto mine. I readjusted my blanket to envelop the both of us the best I could. She was already untying my belt.

"Again?"

I've never said that before and never thought that moment would come, I found myself thinking as soon as I said it aloud.

Her puppy eyes were begging me. "My pussy's aching," she said. "Your big dick is—"

My lips met hers, and I let go of the blanket to wrap my hands around her face. *Let the damn blanket fall as it may.*

I reached under her shirt and untied her bra. As excited as she made me, my cock was not ready for action yet. I motioned for her to stand up, and I did the same before reaching down for the blanket.

After shaking the dirt and leaf debris from it, I placed it flat next to the fire. She followed my cue, leaning back on it. She unbuttoned her shirt and I knelt in between her legs. With her skirt around her waist, I was free to open her legs as wide as I needed them to be. The fire and its shadows turned her already beautiful body into a work of art. Her pussy was glistening wet, again. I licked her inner thighs, worked my way to her clit. I glanced up for a second. She was massaging her tits with one hand, the other arm was folded to prop her head up like a pillow.

I dug in, her pussy juice the perfect dessert to my camping meal. It also turned out to be the cue my cock needed to harden again. I savored her, lightly pinching her labia, then fucking her gently with my tongue and my fingers until she grabbed me by the hair and pulled me back up. I licked her flat stomach on my way to her humongous tits, attending to each as a gentleman should. Then I moved up to her neck and made my way to her mouth, leaving my tongue's wet trail behind.

She kissed me briefly and held my face a couple of inches away from hers, just enough for us to make eye contact.

"Fuck me quietly under the stars," she whispered.

NEXT STEPS

AFTER LEAVING THE CAMPGROUND, I returned my camping equipment, and then dropped off the rental vehicle at the airport.

When Wednesday evening rolled around, I was glad to be boarding a plane again.

Now, don't get me wrong. I'm not complaining. It was a fun camping experience, but my dick needs a break!

I had to say that the past couple of days were one of my best layovers to date.

Even though I didn't get any closer to finding my mystery stewardess, that Tiffany woman proved much more entertaining than most of the random girls I've picked up at bars in the past.

Now comfortably seated in business class, a cold beer in my hand, I try to think of nothing. You could call that my way of meditating, I guess.

I try and resist the urge to pull out the diary, here on the plane. I succeed for now, but my other brain still appears to be controlling the show. I can't help but imagine what each of the female attendants on this flight is like in the sack.

Is one of them *my* stewardess?

I don't even know if she's White, Asian, Black... Maybe she's Hispanic?

Well, at least I know she speaks English.

I change my mind; the temptation is too strong. I can't just sit here and wonder. I dig into my carry-on to retrieve her leather-bound journal.

Maybe if I re-read it one more time I'll find a clue I missed before?

The in-flight blanket carefully placed to cover the large bulge I know will soon appear in my pants, I start studying her detailed account of the all-girl threesome she had with the two hot blondes in Mexico.

They left evidence behind: a sex tape.

Could I potentially get my hands on it?

Would it hold the key that would allow me to uncover her identity?

TO BE CONTINUED...

...IN PART 2 of *The Stewardess's Diary*, available at most major book retailers.

The complete episodic novel is also available in one (thick) paperback with exclusive author's notes about the series and what inspired each episode.

LIST OF EPISODES

The Stewardess's Diary contains ten episodes:

Part 1: Canada introduces the mystery stewardess as a woman who's heartbroken following a disastrous weekend getaway. Alex, a fellow flight attendant on a red-eye flight to Toronto, recommends she stop looking for relationships and instead focus on enjoying the moment, trying out one-night stands. Will the stewardess quiet down her mind and pull it off?

In *Part 2: Mexico*, the stewardess is stranded in Cancun, once again let down by another man. Finding herself without plans at the last minute, she joins two young, beautiful blonde women on their yacht for a quiet afternoon... Or so she thought.

Part 3: Costa Rica sees the stewardess come out of her shell, actively putting herself out there to try and enjoy herself. During a weekend getaway on her own, she signs up for a surf lesson with a handsome instructor. But a surprise awaits them when a cop finds them naked on the beach and makes demands of his own.

In ***Part 4: USA***, while in Los Angeles, the stewardess and one of her friends decide to interview for a publicity campaign promoting an aviation school. They discover what it's like to get screwed—both literally and figuratively—by manipulative, cunning, and good-looking men in L.A.

In ***Part 5: Ireland***, the stewardess heads out on a romantic weekend getaway at an Irish castle with her current boy-toy. But she has no idea that the castle offers such unique *amenities* to their patrons. Butlers, maids, and even guests seem to be at everyone's beck and call.

In ***Part 6: Thailand***, the stewardess explores Bangkok with a fellow flight attendant. While at a spa, she and her coworker experience sensations that most tourists visiting Thailand will never experience. She crosses boundaries that even the captain would never dare touch. Will the captain manage to get closer to the stewardess by tracking down her unique Thai coworker?

In **Part 7: France**, the stewardess goes through a roller-coaster of emotions after learning of her aunt's passing. Her past gets dug up, and she exposes some of her painful romantic memories. Will the identifying details she slipped in her journal be enough for the captain to discover who she is?

In **Part 8: Holland**, the stewardess and one of her co-workers go cycling through the Netherlands and entertain themselves with the handsome men they encounter. The captain believes he may have found her. But did he?

In **Part 9: Japan**, the stewardess participates in a unique Japanese game show. The captain, while trying to track down a copy of that recording, gets himself in deep trouble. Can he find a way to protect his reputation? And will the risk he takes prove to be worthwhile?

In **Part 10: Spain**, the stewardess comes to terms with her sexual desires and leaves a clue behind for the captain to find. Will it be enough for him to finally uncover her identity and meet her?

ABOUT THE AUTHOR

S.M. Pratt is a single woman traveling the world on her own, living in the moment, looking for more than love, and always trying out new things. Fun adventures and unique cultural experiences are always at the top of her agenda, no matter the country she happens to be visiting.

She would love to quit her day job and write full-time. You can help her write the next story faster by purchasing her books and/or giving her five-star reviews. Without your support, she's invisible and unable to make a living doing what she loves, which is creating what you love to read.

If you haven't done so already, please join her private reader group for previews, exclusive offers, and more. It's free: https://smpratt.com

For more information:
smpratt.com
info@smpratt.com